Fire Wolf

By David Evans

Table of Contents

In the early Middle Ages, there lived a sorceress named Ryhs, who loved wolves. One day the town was overrun with fierce rampaging wolves, the king got wind of this and brought in one of his knights along with 3 hunters to hunt down the wolves.

Some of the wolves would stay back and go after the men, while the rest of the wolves made a beeline for the woods.

100 wolves lost their lives, and none of the hunters nor the knight were injured. The king came out of his home to look over the dead wolves and congratulate his men.

No one dared to venture anywhere near the woods for 2 days after the incident. After the second day a lone hunter named

Lionel went into the woods searching for a deer or rabbit to feed his family.

He heard something rustling around and quickly ducked behind a tree, hoping whatever it was didn't see him.

He ever so slowly peeked around and to his surprise it was a wild boar. It was digging up the dirt and rolling around in the soft mud.

He fiercely ran after the boar with his sword, he swung his sword twice and missed the boar twice.

The enraged boar came running after him, he made a run for it into a dark cave. The boar couldn't see him in the dark cave and ran off, Lionel heard someone say you shouldn't be in here.

"Who are you?"

"Your worst nightmare."

I didn't mean to disturb to you, the boar scared me in here.

"Did you hunt down the wolves?"

"No," but my brother did.

Those wolves came from the roodin forest, and someone had let them out of their cages.

I heard that giants live in those woods, that's why I don't go there. One of the wolves was cursed and had particular brown markings around its neck.

"Did you see the dead bodies of the wolves?"

"Yes," and I didn't see the wolf your talking about.

"What are you doing living in here?"

"I'm hiding from the king."

I used to live in the town, but the king ordered his men to chase me out when my sister told them that I was doing magic. I wasn't going to hurt anyone with my magic, now I'm an enemy to the king and the town.

"How long were you practicing magic?"

"For many years."

I used to have the dark elves help me to write my spell books.

"What happened to them?"

"One night they tried to kill me."

I was able to reach my wand, I pointed it at them and said a death spell that killed them. If you make a fire this evening, you'll have to face the evil fire wolf.

He'll ask you three questions, if you answer them incorrectly he'll kill you and your body will turn to flames.

"What are the questions?"

"The first question is whose the knight of Babgonia?"

"Geina."

"The second question is have you hunted the red wolf?"

"You would say no."

"Here's the final question what's the word in the beginning of the wizards riddle?"

"Say the word Shall."

They heard a blood curdling scream; it's sounds like the fire wolf's first victim.

"Will he get stronger if he kills many people?"

"Yes."

After his 12th victim, he'll be able to spit fire like a dragon. The fire wolf very rarely rests.

"How long will he be on fire for after the fire is started?"

"An hour."

If he kills 100 people, he'll be able to stay on fire for 2 hours. He's so powerful that he can melt a Knights armor, in just minutes. Wherever you are, he can hunt you down. Even the largest creature can't win a battle with him.

Be very still, there's an evil giant outside of the cave. It's rather usual for him to be scavenging at this time of day. If you look over by those trees you'll see a red wolf standing there, I still don't see it that's because you aren't focused on it.

You're only focused on the giant; he won't see us as long as you don't raise your voice. Look the boar is in the giants hand, wiggling around trying to get free. The giant took his other hand and broke the boars neck.

That giant has sores, scrapes, and cuts it's because he was fighting with a giant bear. The other day I was walking through the shadow forest collecting several ingredients for my latest experiment.

I could hear that something was coming my way, I quickly went behind a sren tree. If a sren tree feels threatened it'll give you a shock.

The giant saw the red wolf, dropped the half-eaten boar. The wolf snapped its mouth at the giant and went behind a tree stump. Immediately the giant began tearing up the stump, the wolf snarled at him.

A huge log came flying down out of nowhere and slammed into the giant with enough force to knock him over.

That's what you call a tree trap, I haven't seen one of them go off in a long time.

“Do you know the people that set them traps?”

“Yes.”

I saw them last in owl alley, there are 4 of them and their Junna people.

“What does that mean?”

“They are part plant.”

"Do you know what percent plant they are?”

“30.”

That's less than I thought they were. The giant struggled to get to his feet, he grabbed onto a massive vine and was now able to get back on his feet. The red wolf was long gone, a giant land crawler bug went crawling past the cave.

"Have you ever tried riding on the back of one of them?"

"No," I haven't.

I'll tell you what, it was a lot of fun. It tried to bite me several times, I sat back far enough that it couldn't reach me with its large pinchers to bite me.

At one time they almost went extinct, I figured there's three 300 of them left in the wild.

"Have you ever raised one?"

"No," but I know someone that did.

"What was the outcome of that?"

"It wasn't good."

"What was so bad about it?"

"It would chase her around and would try to bite her while she was feeding it."

She told me that she gave it to one of her friends, but her friend soon grew tired of it and killed it 2 weeks later.

"Are red wolves pack animals?"

"Yes," to an extent.

That red wolf that you saw earlier, was the spy of the pack. So that means by the end of today or tomorrow the pack will be coming through here.

They'll probably be looking for food and may try to take shelter in my cave. I've had to fend them off once before, they didn't put up much of a fight.

"Have you been to silver jace land lately?"

"Yes," I have.

The giant owls that live in that land, they have been very unsettled lately. It's because they can sense that fire wolf was awakened, they usually sleep much of the days but now they're on high alert.

They use 5 different kinds of hoots to communicate with one another. I saw one of those owls, attack some sheep.

That's because the sheep interrupted the owls sleep. That's the most aggressive I've seen those owls in a while. I've heard of those owls lay eggs like a chicken, that rumor is true.

I haven't eaten one of those eggs, but they say that they have a foul taste. I'm not going to risk my life to get an egg from those giant owls.

"Do you think the giant owls need to be slayed?"

"No," they just need to be left alone.

"Do those owls ever leave their land?"

"Sometimes but very rarely."

I thought that there were owl hunters that kept the owls in line, there were until the green hoip aliens attacked and killed them. After doing that they flew back into their solar system.

"Did you ever see one of them?"

"No."

The pack of red wolves soon came into view, they're so majestic looking.

Chapter 1: Initiate

Meanwhile Magnus the brother of Lionel was in an intense sword fight with an evil legionnaire in the dark lands. An evil elf came walking by and stopped to watch the men fight.

The legionnaire tried to push him to make him lose his balance, that's when Magnus struck the legionnaire in the arm cutting it clear off. While there were pixies flying from one tree to another.

A giant winged insect, fly by and bumped into one of the 5 pixies. The other pixies stayed back and watched; the pixie got on the back of the insect.

Away they went, they passed through narrow areas. Sometimes they had to fly sideways to avoid the various obstacles.

The pixie closed its tiny eyes, when the insect, landed on the arm of a giant. This didn't seem to bother the giant, he just kept on walking.

Not so long afterwards, the insect now had enough energy to fly around again. The insect flew, into magic vine land. When the vines saw them coming they perked up and began reaching for them.

Sometime later Magnus was able to decapitate the legionnaire, predatory vines were coming towards him. He chopped one of the vines to pieces with his sword, he spun around and struck several more vines.

But these lines were almost solid, so he struck them twice at the same place just to cut through them.

A giant owl flew overhead, luckily it wasn't focused on him. It was on the trail, of its prey. It let out a hoot, that stunned its prey.

This caused his ears to ring; a rabid wolf came out of the woods. He knew just what to do because he delt with the wolves before, the wolf was eyeing him up. The wolf circled around him, snarling, and showing its teeth.

It came closer and he drove his sword into its chest killing it. A few yards away he saw a knight sitting on a tree stump who was looking at something in the woods. He walked over to him, excuse me and the man looked at him.

"What are you doing here?"

"I'm watching for giants."

I'm friends with one of the giants, he's humble and likes to joke around. It's cooling down out here, I'm going to start a fire to stay warm. You don't need to go away, let's talk for a bit.

He began to rub two sticks together; this will take a while to get started. Not if I help you out, no that's alright I can do it. With much frustration, he was able to get the fire started.

"Are you one of the kings men?"

"Yes," I am.

I've been working for him faithfully going on for several years now. The man threw more logs in the fire, to keep it going. Without warning the fire flared up and changed into the shape of a wolf.

Then it began to speak, both men looked at each other with a puzzled look on their faces. Magnus stood up and retreated behind a tree.

"In a low voice the robust fire wolf, asked whose the knight of Babgonia?"

"Geina."

You're just a spirit I'm surprised that you know about him. This is the first time a fire ever talked to me.

"Have you hunted the red wolf?"

"No," I would never think about killing them.

They have become endangered anyway, in a demanding voice he said stop talking and answer my final question.

"What's the word in the beginning of the wizards riddle?"

"I don't know."

The fire wolf immediately roared and lunged forward and fiercely tore into his body leaving his body engulfed in flames.

The fire wolf stopped feeding on the knight and began wandering around looking for more possible prey.

When the pixies saw the bright flames they retreated back into their tree homes. Everything around the wolf was catching fire, even the smallest of ground creatures seeked cover.

A yeti came to the scene, it began pelting the fire wolf with big rocks. Most of the rocks just melted the fire wolf said you pathetic brave creature you surly will die. Go back to your dwelling at once, let me be.

I'm looking for humans to prey on. You look like a hairy human, and you don't talk. You don't have enough brains to even talk.

The fire wolf brushed up against a sren tree, it felt the heat and immediately let out an intense shock. This only infuriated the wolf causing him to *roar* out.

He walked on for half a mile and soon came to a creek teeming with various wildlife. The shiny shelled diamond crabs crawled along on the rocks.

A fox was hiding out in the tall grass, that grew on the side of the creek. A snapping turtle climbed up out of the water and was sitting close to a diamond crab.

These animals had never saw a fire wolf and were afraid of him. The snapping turtle quickly retreated back into its shell; the diamond crabs quickly dove into the water.

The fox retreated back deeper into the woods and felt at ease once again. The pixies watched from above, their bodies tensed up because of their fear of the wolf.

The spitting fish swam over by where the wolf was and spit water in his face, this caused him to back away from the water. Nearby there was a crossbow warrior who was lost, he had lost sight of the king.

He stood behind a tree, as he watched the fire wolf. A pixie that was in the tree that the man stood behind had started to laugh at the joke the other pixie was saying to him.

The wolf immediately turned around and was focused on the tree, it could sense that something was there.

It grew angered at the incessant laughing pixie and shot a fireball at it. The branches where the pixie was caught fire, so the pixie flew away from the tree and collided with a blue bird in midair.

The pixie was disoriented and flew down into the water. The wolf snarled and this only scared the pixie even more, a pixie mother came out of nowhere and took the pixie away to safety.

The man squeezed the trigger on the crossbow, releasing a bolt that flew right through the fire wolf. The wolf immediately ran towards the tree.

The man immediately climbed up on top of a tall boulder. The wolf growled and attempted to jump up at the man but fell short.

This gave the man enough time to reload his crossbow, and fire again. His arrow passed through the wolf and did nothing to stop it.

The wolf jumped up and was now able to get up on the boulder. The man jumped down off the boulder and ran as fast he could through the woods. He dropped his crossbow but kept going anyway. The wolf was hot on his trail, there was no escape.

He soon entered the giant fern forest; he ran past a wizard who was practicing his spells.

Exhaustion set in and the man collapsed onto the home of a pixie, luckily the pixie was able to escape.

Chapter 2: Excursion

The fire wolf left the wizard in awe, he thought this must be a new species of wolf.

He stood up and his elbow accidently bumped a potion container causing to fall to the ground and explode. The blast threw him into a tree, knocking him out.

The wolf ignored the wizard and went after the man, once it came upon him it devoured him. The man's body was engulfed in flames, his body burned until it was gone.

Soon after this the fire wolf's flame burned out and he disappeared. Magnus went back to his home; his sister was there feeding there horse.

"What are you doing all this time?"

"Exploring."

I saw something in those woods, that left me afraid. I don't want you going into the forest alone anymore, it's not like you to say something like that. If you enjoy living then I suggest you listen.

"Did what you see come after you?"

"No."

I observed it in action, it attacked a knight and burned him to death. It asked him three questions, and very aggressively attacked him. It was a wolf that was on fire, it was very unusual.

"Do you think it's a curse?"

"I'm not sure."

I'm surprised that Lionel isn't here tending to the chickens. I collected several chicken eggs; those will be for breakfast tomorrow.

"Have you talked to the goat farmer?"

"Yes," I have.

Something broken into the goat enclosure, killing two of his goats. He said that it was the work of a red wolf, he even showed me the footprints. He asked me to make a partridge for his hailing uncle.

I made it for him while you were away, it didn't take long. You should think about telling the king about this, I'm not even sure he would believe me.

I'm sure that he would send out a team to look for this thing, yes but I'm afraid they'll die.

I'm starting to get worried about your brother, he always tells me never to worry about him. If he comes back, I'll make sure he stays here.

"Where's your mother?"

"She's at the creek washing our clothes."

"How long ago did she leave?"

"Just a few minutes ago."

I better go pay her a visit, it's not good for her to be at the creek.

"How long ago have you been to the dark forest?

"A few days ago."

I hope that you were with someone, Lionel was with me.

"Did you say hello to the pixies while in the forest?"

"No," I didn't.

Your brother always tells me not to, there's nothing wrong with talking to them.

"Did he take you past the wizard dwellings in giant fern forest?"

"No."

"Have you ever been passed the fern forest?"

"No," I haven't.

"Is there something that you want me to see there?"

"'No," I was just asking.

Lionel was telling me about when he escaped a giant, it was a thrilling story. Giants are extremely dangerous; you could easily get killed by them.

Don't let him convince you to go see one, I'll never forgive him if something happens to you.

They heard a disturbance by the horse barn, and quickly ran out to see what was going on.

There were 2 men having a fist fight, several people were gathered around them. Let's go back inside, it’s too noisy out there.

Back in the cave Lionel was still talking with the sorceress, it's been nice talking to you. My sister is probably wondering what I'm doing.

Safe travels, thanks. Lionel was making his way through the shadow forest, the pixies were singing, the rainbow birds were happily chirping up a storm.

There was an evil elf, holding his hatchet while walking along. Lionel just ignored the elf and went on his merry way. He hadn't been to haron lake in a while, so he headed in that direction.

Suddenly flying insects came flying in, one of them tried to fly off with him but he beat them down. He found himself trying to escape, but he bumped into a fox.

The fox let out a yip and ran off. His one foot fell down into shallow a hole, he could hear a hissing insect nearby. He was able to free up his foot and got out of there before the insect came for him.

He soon came to the lake, the zygon fish were swimming alongside flying sea horses. Lightning struck the water, and this spooked them, the fish were trying to find cover in the sunken rocks.

After a bit the sky cleared up, and everything was calm again. He could still hear the chirps from the rainbow birds.

He stood up and walked away from the lake, and headed home. This time he was careful where he stepped. There was a barking monkey above him somewhere in the treetops.

To his surprise the monkey came down from the tree and began doing sign language in front of him.

I'm not sure what you're trying to tell me, it brought up its arms and walked around awkwardly.

> "Are you trying to tell me that a giant is coming?"
>
> "The monkey shook it's head Yes."

The monkey put his hand in his mouth, you're being a crazy monkey.

"What are you trying to tell me now?"

"The monkey pretended to knawel on his arm"

"Are you telling me that the giant is a cannibal"

"He shook his head Yes."

I'd spend more time with you, but I need to get home. Lionel pointed to the top of the tree; you need to go back up there.

Instead of listening to him, the monkey threw pieces of fruit at him. He high tailed it out of there and reached the valley where his home was.

Chapter 3: Alistair & Gatlin

He walked down the muddy path and went over to his house. He opened the door; his sister was standing there with an angry look on her face.

Your brother stormed out of here, it's not going to be easy to calm him down. He went away to check on our mother.

He keeps on telling me about this mysterious beast, he said that it's a wolf that's on fire that disturbs everything that dwells in the woods.

I was hoping that you knew something about it too, I do know a lot about it.

"Who told you about it?"

"A sorceress."

"What's her name?"

"Ryhs"

You're not supposed to talk to them, you could have gotten in trouble. The king knew that they are trouble and kicked one out of here. I'm wondering what your brother is going to say about all this.

I don't think he'll be pleased with you; he's been doing jobs for the king. I wouldn't bow down to him, like my brother does.

He doesn't want you going anywhere for the rest of the day, he made it clear to me several times.

"What was something that you discussed with her?"

"Things about her life."

You don't need to be afraid to tell me anything, we talked about spells and about the creatures that reside in the forest.

"Would you say she's smarter than us?"

"No."

She just lives differently than we do, we live in a house, and she lives in a cave.

"Does she have leprosy?"

"No."

I thought that all sorceries have that, that's not true. While they were talking wizards Alistair and Gatlin were plotting to take the sorceress hostage.

There best friend is a prisoner in owl land and only the sorceress can undo the spell that keeps him imprisoned.

We should take her captive today; I'm almost done making the sleeping tonic that were going to give to her.

"What if she wakes up?"

"Then we'll tie her to a tree."

There are a few walking trees there, I thought that they went extinct.

"What's your plan if the giant owls come after us?"

"Then we'll fire our defense spell at them."

I didn't think that was a strong enough spell to stop them, it sure was. Remember when I saved you from the owl that tried to fly away with you. Yes, vaguely. To stop the owl that day, I used the fire spell.

That owl lost many of its feathers and retreated into the wicked forest of darkness.

"Do you think it got out of there alive?"

"No."

Everything in their tries to kill you and is evil. I won't even go near that place; the flowers shoot barbs at you. There are vines in there that crawl around like a snake and have a mouth like a Venus fly trap. One time a shepherd asked me to go into that forest and find one of sheep that went in there.

I refused to go in there, he was furious with me and went in there himself. Him nor the sheep ever came out of their again.

I'm sure that many things in there attacked them both because they had nothing to defend themselves with.

"Did the shepherds family know about it?"

"No."

"Do you think she'll know that we're coming?"

"No."

"Should we bring a giant along with us?"

"I don't see the need for that."

"Where did you put my wand?"

"I'm not sure."

You're good at losing my stuff, I don't appreciate it. That was a special wand, you'll be helping me find that.

We shouldn't be looking for it now, yes we should. It could be under the caldron, I just looked it's not there.

“Where else do you think it is?”

“In my room.”

You know that I don't like going in there, it's always a mess. If you can't find it I'll just get you a new wand.

He stepped on a frog while he was searching. There's too many frogs around here, I don't know where they all came from.

It's because you kept on saying that spell wrong, you were probably saying the frog attractant spell.

You're always rushing around; you need to slow yourself down. You knocked over my water cup two times, among countless other things.

"Do you know what's growing in that tree beside the house?"

"Yes," it's a stinging beetles nest.

Then we need to get rid of them at once, there a good protector for our home. Our roof is still damaged from that dive bird attack. You weren't here when it happened, I don't even remember where you were.

"How many of them were there?"

"15 of them."

"Did you kill them?"

"Some of them."

"Did you go outside after them?"

"No."

I just opened the window and pointed my wand out the window at them.

"What spell did you say?"

"The personal protection spell."

"How many times did you have to say it?"

"Just twice."

"Did you know that those type of bird had teeth?"

"No."

"Do you think someone sent them after you?"

"Yes," I do.

It was that evil elf that we fought the other day. Through the years we must have fought hundreds of those elves.

I don't understand what makes them so mean. The best answer I have for you is that's how they're born.

We always have a good time when we hang out with the good elves. One time the elves offered you a beer, then you drank it after I told you not to. You were sick for three days after that, and very irritable.

Every little thing would set you off, and I had to walk away. I had the fairy mother and muna the half elf human take care of you.

I don't even remember that they definitely took good care of you because you're still here. Muna said that you were very moody and crazy, you and I are definitely crazy.

"Have you seen that jar of Meeta fruit?"

"No," I haven't.

I've just been having a craving for that fruit lately; I hope you didn't eat it and not tell me. I wouldn't do something like that, I don't believe you.

Now you're going to say that a fruit snake took it away, you're unbelievable. You look so dumbfounded; I don't want to argue with you.

Last week I gave the local garbage snake some rotten fruit, and it tried to bite me. They need to find a different garbage snake for the job.

"Has it ever tried to bite you before?"

"No."

Maybe it didn't like what you gave it, but they accept any trash. Maybe someone forgot to give it it's nectar, to keep it calm. This world we live in is so upside down, sometimes I wonder how were still sane.

A gargoyle bat swooped down after them, get out of here you silly bat. Don't make us, say a spell.

You look so ridiculous holding that broom and chasing that bat out of here. I'm going to make you in charge of getting rid of the next bat.

"Where do those bats live anyway?"

"They live by the lake in a cave."

Chapter 4: Mission

We should go back to the lake sometime; I don't know when we would find the time. I can never remember the name of that lake if you don't remember I'll tell you. We need to keep our eyes peeled for salamanders; we'll be using them for our next potion.

“Is our pack loaded and ready to go?”

“Yes.”

They headed out in search of the sorceress; I'm hoping that we can find her in the cave. They saw an elf trying to start a fire, he looks like he needs help.

We don't have time to start a fire. Just as they were walking away, the elf got the fire started.

The fire wolf came out of the fire, and this time didn’t ask it’s questions and chased after the elf.

The elf quickly began to climb up a tree, the fire wolf went near the tree setting it a blaze. This upset the dive birds that were resting on the branches of the tree.

One of them tried to go after the elf, but he stood his ground and fought it off. Both Wizards happened to look back and saw the large tree ablaze.

I wonder what happened to that tree, who knows. Look there's an animal running around on fire, no that's no ordinary animal that's a fire wolf.

"Haven't you ever read about the legend of the fire wolf?"

"No."

It's known to be a very vicious creature that destroys everything in its path. Don't ever approach it, or you'll surely die.

"Can't we stop it?"

"No."

Neither one of us know how to break its curse, so we're going to leave it alone.

"Do you think it went after that elf?"

"I'm sure that it did."

It's not fussy about what it goes after. Take your eyes off the fire wolf and let's go, I know that your mesmerized by the wolf but come on this way.

Soon the fire wolf's fire will go out and will disappear until the next fire is lit. Step over that spider nest and watch out for the bat. Then the bat landed on his arm, get off me you creepy animal. Don't just watch me struggle with his bat help me, thanks for getting that bat away from me.

It's no big deal it was just a bat, maybe to you it wasn't a big deal but I'm afraid of them.

When I was younger I was exploring a different cave and little did I know that there would be a swarm of bats coming after me.

I don't know how you can enjoy a cave, it's dark, cold, and ugly inside. Plus, there's a chance you may get stuck in there, then who's going to know if you're stuck.

A chicken ran past them squawking, I haven't saw a chicken for so long. You should think about trying to raise some, I don't have the interest to.

Stop moving and look up, I just heard a squawk from a dive bird. We have to get serious now if it sees any movement it'll attack.

After some time passed, the bird didn't see them and finally moved on. I can't believe we stood still back there for so long, we were just playing it safe.

Next time I'm not going to stop for those birds, when you get pecked on the head by those birds don't come crying to me. When they come down after me, I'll just whack them with a stick.

They could feel the ground shaking, there's no reason to be alarmed it's just a giant.

"When do you think our giant is up to?"

"He's probably causing trouble somewhere knowing him."

I thought that you taught him better than that, no that's just how he is. I'm afraid he's going to get killed one of these days by a giant trap.

The likelihood of that happening is very minimal, he knows where the traps are set by now. I showed him where the traps were many times.

"Did he ever try to carry you around?"

"Yes."

I don't let him do that with me anymore, it scares me. Soon they reached the cave, she may have special traps around the cave. Watch out for any foot snares, there could even be spell traps.

"Do you see any movement in the cave?"

"No," not at the moment.

Keep in mind she may come out of there to anytime; we must be ready.

"Do you know which spells you're going to say?"

"Yes," I do.

Just act normal when we approach her, we don't want her thinking that were up to something. Say hello, and we'll ask her how she's doing.

Remember to keep the conversation short, we want to get in there and get out. They carefully approached the entrance to the cave; you have to look wherever you go.

The foot snares could have some dirt over them camouflaging them. If you get your foot stuck on one of those and break it, that'll surely be the end of you.

A bat swooped down from the ceiling of the cave chasing after a bug. These are such narrow spaces in here, quit complaining you're the one that said you like caves.

I just don't like the inside of this cave; you crack me up. I think that we should have went right back there when we went left.

Don't second guess yourself you're going the right way; it won't be much longer until we reach the back in the cave.

If you keep talking quiet enough she won't hear us. There's a whole lot of flies in here, they keep trying to land on me.

If these flies don't drive anyone out of here I don't know what will. Finally, they spotted her, sitting next to her cauldron with a red wolf sitting near her.

"Do you think she's going to recognize us?"

"I'm sure that she will."

I don't like the sight of that wolf, hopefully she doesn't have it attack us. I'm sure everything will go just fine, maybe in a perfect world. They walked out into the opening, and Rhys saw them.

It's been so long since I've seen the both of you, we thought that we would come and say hello. You don't have to be nervous around the wolf, it's very old and slow.

This wolf has been with me for a long time, and mostly allows everyone to pet him. We caught a glimpse of the fire wolf, but we kept our distance.

"Do you know who created that beast?"

"Yes," I made it.

Something must have really made you mad to make you make that beast. The both of you can sit down if you'd like, no we're okay.

That fire wolf is stirring up trouble out there, maybe it'll make the king think about what he did to me. Don't worry we aren't very fond of the king either, he just looks down upon us.

He doesn't want us using our magic when around him. He’s very demanding to his men and can be very arrogant. He has more riches than all of us and is still looking for more.

Chapter 5: Mastermind

He’s only going to rule for another year, I'll just be glad when he's gone. While she was busy, they took out sleepy dust from their pockets and blew it towards her with some air from their mouths.

She yawned and fell over and so did her wolf. This is going as planned, our friend will be so glad to get out of owl land.

We really should have another person with us, this isn’t going to be easy. We're going to get her very carefully out of here, watch where you're walking.

There are some sharp rocks in here, you don't want one of them going into your ankle.

We should do the carrying spell, that way she'll float up in the air and follow us. He spoke the spell and before there very eyes she floated up into the air just above them. You better watch that she doesn't bump into anything.

We don't want any harm coming to her, some bats flew overhead. They carefully stepped over some jagged rocks, and we're now leaving the cave.

I'm just glad to be out of that cave, me as well. I thought for sure she was going to bump her head back there.

They walked down a path, if any people see us there going to think we're crazy. If they ask us who's that floating person, and I would breakout in laughter.

They could hear the rainbow birds chirping, I wish there were more friendly birds around here. Those dive birds are ugly and their territorial.

If you dislike them that much then you should go hunt them down. I wouldn’t want to waste my time doing that, but you could.

The lake looks so nice from here, but we must be on our way. I haven't swam in that lake for a long time. I think that owl world gets further and further away, no it's just because were tired.

We'll be coming up on the warped bridge that leads us there soon. I like how the good elves put torches along this trail, the fire spell keeps them lit forever.

Eventually they crossed the warped bridge, they could hear the owls doing there roaring hoots.

I don't know about you, but these hooting sounds are very annoying. I'm glad that we have reached the jail, there friend was lying down resting.

"Shall we wake her up now?"

"No," but soon.

"Do you think the owls are going to attack us right now?"

"No," but there's always a chance that they will.

It looks like the owls are getting closer to us, just don't move and they won't see you. That owl back there is an old one, and I've witnessed it being in many fights with the other owls.

"Have you ever had one swooped down after you?"

"Yes," but amazingly I escaped.

I dislike these owls just as much as you do. Now we're going to wake her up, it was just five minutes ago that you told me not to wake her up.

Make up your mind and keep thinking. You go ahead and do the spell; I'm watching our backs.

These owls will sometimes sneak up from behind you, I don't think they're going to do that right now.

Go ahead, he walked over to Rhys and said the awake spell. A minute later she opened her eyes and didn't recognize where she was.

"'What happened to me I'm out of my cave?"

"We were all taken here to owl land."

You're just trying to smooth things over and tell me a story. You both kidnapped me, it's unacceptable.

It's not like we hurt you or anything, I don't care, it still doesn't give you the right.

"Why did you take me here anyway?"

"For you to undo a difficult spell."

"What did you do with my wolf?"

"We did nothing to him, he's still back in the cave."

I wish I could call in the fire wolf and tell him to go after the both of you. That's a real nice thing to say to us, and our friend got put in the jail in here.

If he acts like you two do I can see why he's in there. To get rid of the spell it may take me awhile, hopefully you're okay with that.

I swear one of those owls are eyeing us up, don't worry about them we'll keep them away from you.

I refuse to sleep in this place, we should leave here before it gets dark. If not then we'll be dealing with the evil nightcrawlers, who will relentlessly come after us.

That owl over there is certainly moving around a lot, maybe the spiders are getting on it. If one of these owls falls over it will crush us all, we know that.

Then she got started on the spell, not so far away from them stood a walking tree. It's good to see that walking tree here, it will give us more protection. Don't think about trying to run away from us, it won’t work.

"Is there anything else you want me to do after this?"

"No."

Don't let your friend come back here, we won't. A lone dive bird began going after one of the owls.

The owl mediately pecked the bird knocking him down. That owl certainly took care of business quick, I'm afraid it's going to do it to us.

"Why don't you make a defense bubble spell?"

"I'm sure that I could."

He spoke the spell and the defense bubble wrapped around them.

"Do you feel much safer now?"

"Yes," I do.

Suddenly one of the old owls, took off into the air and a young owl collided with him. We better get ready to run if that owl falls down here. I haven't seen them fight in midair for a while, they're probably just having a disagreement.

"Over what do you think?"

"They're probably fighting over food."

She doesn't look very happy over there, she'll get over it. She won't be leaving until the job is done.

"What are you chewing on?"

"Sugar Cain."

Suddenly there was an explosion, and the sorceress was lying there in shock. When they saw her they came running, she doesn't look so good.

"Can you hear us?"

"There was no answer."

The gate to the jail was open, and there friend was relieved. The sorceress woke up, but her ears were ringing. You're so glad that you're alright, we weren't sure what happened to you.

Whomever created that spell, put a surprise in it. If I was any closer to the gate I would have been killed by the explosion. The ground began to shake, which disrupted the owls and a large crack formed in the warped bridge.

Chapter 6: Encounters

After the quake was over, one of the wizards went over to check on the warped bridge.

What he saw concerned him, there was a deep crack in the bridge and several other smaller cracks. He went back to tell the others what he had saw.

"How's the bridge looking?"

"It's in rough shape."

We'll have to cross it one person at a time, because it's too weak to hold all of our weights.

An evil giant came out of nowhere, when the owls seen him they flew over and began attacking him.

The giant tried to grab the owls, but they were too quick for him. They're sharp talons tore into his skin, making him scream out.

I don't care about the one-person rule about the bridge anymore, let's just get out of here. They all ran across the bridge, parts of the bridge collapsed.

"What are we going to do about the bridge?"

"We'll fix it later."

For now, we have to get the sorcerer's back to the cave safely.

"Do you think more giants are going to come after us?"

"No," I don't think so.

Their friend was walking along and collapsed, I don't think I have the strength to go on much further. Don't give up on us now, we're almost there.

I have to eat something to gain my strength back, but there's no food around.

The both of you are wizards, I'm sure you know of a food spell.

You're in luck because I found a thunder Berry Bush over here. The last time that we tried to do a food spell it went terribly wrong. It sounds like you both haven't been practicing your spells enough.

If you'd like we'll teach you about spells, no I have no need to learn them. They handed him a handful of thunder berries, these are nice and ripe. I should buy the seed for these berries and grow them myself.

"Does anyone here know where I can buy the seeds?"

"No," we don't.

After eating the berries, he stood up and they continued on their way. I’m parched with thirst if it ain’t one thing it's another with you.

Can’t you all be less critical with me, I was kept locked up for a few days, I just can't help it.

When we get to the lake, you can drink all that you want. Don't ask how far the lake is from here because none of us know that.

“Where did you get that cut on your arm?”

“From a dive bird.”

I did kill the bird, but it wasn't easy.

"What were you fed while you were in jail?"

"Pieces of bread."

I think the bread was a few days old, the evil elves didn't care or did they have any remorse for me.

"Did they say much to you?"

"No."

The nights in that jail were the worst, the owls hooted all night. I repeatedly told the elves to make the owls be quiet and they just laughed at me.

That evening I smacked one of the elves for talking smart to me, I never saw him again.

I think those berries have made me thirsty, I've never heard of them causing you to get thirsty.

"Why are you grabbing rocks for?"

"There are some giant earth crawlers coming this way, you really shouldn't be throwing rocks at them."

You're not there rule maker, just let me throw some rocks. They all walked on ahead of him, he's acting like a child. If he gets attacked by them, it's his own.

We're only telling him things for his own good. In a minute he's going to be surrounded by them, and he won't know what to do.

I thought that the time he spent in jail would have made him more appreciative of things. That's because some people never learn, like him for instance.

Their friend grabbed a sharp object and began cutting up the crawlers. He killed several of them and caught back up with his pals.

"Did you get hurt by them?"

"No," I slaughtered them.

There's too many of them, and I dislike them because there so noisy. Some people like to ride on the backs of those bugs, to me that's just weird.

Look at all those pixies in that tree, they certainly look happy intermingling with one another.

I sometimes wish that I had a simple life like they do, but my life is full of endless tasks.

"Have any of you had a pixie for a pet?"

"No," we haven't.

"Can we talk about something more intelligent?"

"Yes," we can.

"Does anyone know who the new kings going to be?"

"No," we don't follow that.

They soon came to the lake, I'm so glad to see that water. Without thinking he went into the lake and was splashing around. I hope that he quiets down or he’s going to attract water flies.

If they come out I'm getting out of here, they sting and bite. If I hear any buzzing, that means that they're on their way.

I never get in that lake, not after my friend was killed by the water flies. That swarm of water flies was the biggest one I've ever seen. My friend killed most of them but there stings eventually killed him.

“Are you done splashing around in there?”

“Yes,” I am.

I appreciate you guys allowing me to stop here, the water tasted so good in my dry mouth. We thought maybe you were bathing yourself in there too, I wouldn't do that in front of you guys.

Don't move there are 2 warrior witch's going past us, and one of them happened to turn and saw them.

"What do we do now?"

"Let the sorceress take care of it."

The wizards stood together ready to say a spell, the sorceress and the witch began fighting.

"What if she losses?'

"Then we run like maniacs."

The sorceress fired a ball of fire at the witch, but the witch quickly deflected it with a defensive spell. The sorceress created a ball of electricity and fired it at the witch.

This knocked the witch to the ground and electricity was pulsing through her. The other witch ran off, but the sorceress caught up with her.

The sorceress fired acid rain and a ball of electricity, once both collided it made a huge explosion killing the witch. The sorceress returned to them; they were all clapping for her. We've never seen such powerful magic and spells used; it wasn't easy. That battle tired me out when I get back I'm going to rest. Sometime later they came to her cave, they all said their goodbyes and the wizards and there friend went home. Lionel and his sister got done with their conversation and afterwards his brother came back with their mother. It's good to see you mom, it's good to see you all too. Your brother was telling me of a mysterious beast.

"Have both of you saw this beast?"

"No," just Magnus did.

Chapter 7: Adventure

Their mother immediately began preparing a meal for them. I checked our garlic plants; they seem to be growing quite well. Someday I want each of you to have your own garden.

Don't ask the fairies for help, you need to figure it out on your own. I'm going to give each of you a different seed, I'm looking forward to seeing all your plants grow.

"When do you want us to do that?"

"In several months."

"If you don't mind, my brother and I are going to have a conversation outside."

"Don't forget to come back in here and have your dinner, we won't."

"What do you think we should do about the beast?"

"Have the zar wizard kill it."

We need to go to him as soon as possible before more lives are going to be lost. The last time that we visited him, he showed us a dragon egg.

I'm wondering if the dragon ever hatched, I'm sure that it did.

"Do you remember that spell that he taught us?"

"Yes," If do.

I can't believe that one time you asked him if he was grandfather, that only seemed to irritate him. I think that he got that way because he was tired.

He does have a nice grandson, him and I have had long conversations. We better head in there, I'm sure dinner is about ready.

When they walked in their mother came over to them, you're both just in time. I made my famous apple marinated pig, the last time that you made that it was really good. Everyone took a seat, and we're ready to dig in when a stranger walked in. My home was burned down when a beast attacked my house.

"Do any of you know where the king is?"

"No," we don't.

I better be going now, what a rude fella. Tomorrow for dinner we're having chicken legs, I have plenty of bread for all.

These apples are so sweet, I've had this pig cooking on a spit for hours, I'm glad to see everyone is enjoying it.

This meat is extra tender, and the apples topped this off. I’m teaching your sister cooking skills, she's a fast learner.

I had the pig roasting over the fire, you can't keep doing that. The fire wolf will surely find you, but I’m wondering why it didn't come out of the fire after you. Maybe it's because of the potion that I drank. That could have something to do with it.

“What was in that potion drink?”

“Ground up Barley, garlic, and grinded up spider.”

“What kind of spider was it?”

"A magic spider."

I know where there are plenty of them. I bet the magic spider is the key to keeping it away, but I'm going to ask the wizard anyway.

I see that everyone enjoyed their meal, you should start making your homemade soup again.

Making that soup takes a lot of time and effort, I'm tired just from cooking. The older I get the less I want to do, that's why I'm teaching all of you now how to cook among other skills. It's okay we all still love you: you sure know how to make me feel better.

Their sister stood up, allow me to help you with the dishes. Boys, please tell your sister that she doesn't have to do the dishes every night.

Their mother remained sitting there, their sister collected their plates and was now on her way to the creek.

Were surprised she isn't afraid to go down to the creek alone. It's because she's used to doing it so much, that danger no longer enters her mind.

I don’t like to do this, but I need to go lay down, have a good night everyone. Then their sister came back, she had a perplexed look on her face. That was one interesting trip to the creek, I'm just glad I was able to help somebody.

“What happened at the creek?”

"A child had fallen in the creek and was drowning."

I dropped the dishes and quickly grabbed the boy out of the water. You're such a help to everyone, the people around here do appreciate what I do for them.

While our neighbor was on his walking trip, I took care of his horses. That was very rewarding, he gave me a gold coin.

"Did you spend it yet?"

"No," I didn't.

"Are the both of you going somewhere?"

"Yes."

Don't worry I'm not going to tell your mother; she's been needing a lot more rest lately.

I just don't like seeing her this way, hopefully she's better tomorrow. While you're gone I'm going to go see my boyfriend.

"How's he been doing lately?"

"He's doing alright."

The other day that I was with him, he was telling me about his adventures in the forests.

He sounds like a rather independent individual, but he does like to talk lot. He's a handsome young man, and he always treats me well.

I hope that you enjoy your time away from here, we will. As they were walking along the path, they saw some giant Earth crawlers. You and I know better not to mess around with those crawlers.

Off to their left there was a man cutting down a tree, there were some young children standing around taking in the sights. It's good to see children out here, I don't think so.

“Why not?”

“That fire wolf is roaming around.”

Who knows where it's going to come out next, were going to put an end to its reign soon. I hope that we don't see any more witches, I don't think so.

They should lock them all up, that's not fair. When they’re around everyone is in danger, I don't see the good that they do. They keep the beasts away, but they're mean.

There mean so that people stay away from them, they can't focus with people around.

“Did you realize that the king hunts for witches and evil creatures in his free time?”

“No,” I didn't realize that.

They came upon a rainbow bird nest, look at all the baby birds. I don’t see the mother or father bird, I'm sure they're around somewhere.

We should take one of these and make it our pet, just leave them alone. Besides that, we don't have the time to raise a bird, you wouldn't know what to feed it.

They soon came to a creek, the last time that I tried crossing this creek I slipped on a slippery rock and fell in. Just take it slow, you'll make it across.

If you're unsure come over here where I am, it's easier to cross here. He went over there and easily crossed the creek.

The water sure is flowing quickly down the creek, that's a good thing because the critters in here like that.

They entered the giant fern forest; this is such a mystical place.

"'Have you ever camped out in this place?"

"No."

Your just not that adventurous, you don't realize how dangerous the creatures are that come out at night around these parts.

You wouldn't last very long overnight, after a few minutes you'd be running for your life.

If I saw the creatures I'd try to kill them, that wouldn't be wise thing to do. You don't want them tearing you limb from limb. I'm not so sure that's how they would kill you, just believe me they would.

Chapter 8: Together

Some of the predators are like pack hunters, these creatures run around on two legs like we do. They're hunters not scavengers, there's a thunder berry bush over there.

We should pick some of them, I'm too full and can't eat another thing. I don't know where you're putting at all.

It's not going to be for me. I'm going to give them to the wizard, that's very nice of you.

"What burrowed that hole over here?"

"One of the nighttime creatures."

"How many different species of nighttime creatures are there around these parts?"

"4 different species."

"Are all of them very aggressive?"

"Yes."

"Why can't the creatures just be happy around here?"

"Because they're angry, and don't know how to be nice to other creatures."

They arrived at the wizard's place; he always keep this place looking nice. I don't know why there's always so many pixies in his yard, that's because they can sense his good energy.

He used to have a beautiful weeping Willow tree in his backyard, until the tree rats came along.

"You've seen those before haven't you?"

"Not that I recall."

They only seem to go after that kind of tree, if you look closely at the ground you'll see their tracks. I see them, but I'm not going to follow them.

"Can you explain to me what they look like?"

"They have a long neck and a plump body."

Their teeth are so large that they hang out of their mouth, with small eyes. The wizard saw them there and came out to greet them, I'm glad to see you both here today. Lionel offered him some thunder berries, go ahead, and take some. I haven't had one of these berries in a long while.

"What are the both of you here for?"

"For some help and advice."

Let's talk about this inside, my dragon hatched since the last time you have visited. He's a friendly dragon, but sometimes he tries my patience. You certainly have a lot of things in here, I'm trying to make room for new things.

"Is your dragon in here?"

"Yes," but it's sleeping.

Take a seat in here, let me know about all your troubles. I don't know if you've ever heard of this beast before, it's called a fire wolf.

I know what you're talking about, I have several legend books, it talks about the fire wolf in one of those.

"Do you know who created it?"

"Yes."

"Was it a sorceress?"

"Yes."

She created the wolf out of anger towards the king. I watched it kill someone, it scared me to the core. The more people that it kills the stronger it gets.

"Do magic spiders keep him away?"

"Yes."

But after just three days the magic spiders spell wears off, that's when he'll return. When I was a young man, this area was terrorized by a fire wolf.

It was so bad, and I had to move out of here for a while, or at least until the fire wolf went away.

"Do you know who defeated the fire wolf before?"

"No."

I wonder how long it takes to defeat the fire wolf, it's a difficult process.

"Where did this fire wolf dwell?

"Anywhere."

That sounds odd to me, usually it stays in one area. Something in that curse must have changed, but I'm not sure what. Only one person can hunt this fire wolf down.

I'm reluctant to fight it, maybe your dragon could assist you. The last dragon I had I would take him with me into battle. He could turn anyone into a blaze, quicker than they could defend themselves.

"Have you battled with any witches?"

"Yes," plenty of times.

They may know a lot of magic but not many strong spells. My parents did practice magic and spells, and we're very good at using spells.

They passed down everything that they know to me, I know all kinds of magic and every speller there is.

You shouldn't fight the fire wolf at night because he'll be twice as strong. Tomorrow I'll start my search for him, hopefully he'll be around here somewhere. I know that it asks you three questions.

"Do you know why it does that?"

"Because those thoughts were on her mind when she created him."

What I mean is she was thinking about the knight, she was also thinking about the red wolves and riddles.

"Then what made them into the form of questions?"

"The fire wolfs evil spirit."

Now it's starting to make more sense to me. They spotted a golden wand that was on top of a big book.

"Where did you get that wand?"

"It was my father's."

"Can we take a look at it?"

"Sure, you can, just don't drop it."

They picked it up and were carefully looking it over. There were several grooves in the wand, he carefully pressed in one of them. The back of the wand opened up, there was a folded-up piece of paper inside.

"Have you ever opened up the wand?"

"No."

They handed the paper to the wizard, he carefully unraveled it. He took out his glasses and put them on and began reading it.

It says dear son, I hope this letter finds you well. As you may know I have traveled to magic land.

Your mother and I were looking at wands, we looked them over for a while and chose this very wand.

Use this wand well, and you'll always have something from me with you. Your mom and I love you very much, stay strong my son.

Tears began running down his chapped cheeks, my father always knew how to write a good letter.

They walked into another room, where they found a glowing blue crystal ball. I wouldn't touch that If I were you.

We'll ask the wizard first before handling it, we don't want to break any of this stuff. We should see what's at the bottom of the steps over here.

Don't think about it, just come over here. We may find something unique down there, well probably just find his dragon down there. We shouldn't hang out in his basement without his permission.

It's something happens to us it's on you, I know. Together they walked down the steps, he even has a candle lit for us.

I think he just forgot to put it out. I wouldn't go to the dark side of the basement; I don't think there's anything there. The baby dragon is there, it appears to be sleeping. If you touch it you're going to wake it up. He couldn't reach us anyway because he's got a chain connected to his leg.

Look at it his wings, he has some big teeth. Just then the wizard came down the steps, I see that the both of you have found my dragon. He's a very mellow dragon and is lazy.

I'm sorry it took me so long to come over, it was such a heartfelt letter. I don't like to spend much time down here, it's dark and chilly. You should spend more time with your dragon, I do.

We don't like that he's tied down with chains, sometimes he can get a little unruly.

One time he coughed, and some fire came out of his mouth. I keep all my papers and books away from him. He munched on several in my books before, but he's got to learn.

Let's get out of this basement now, I'll tend to the dragon later. He showed them into another room, this is where the both of you will be sleeping tonight. If you get hungry you can have some leftover bread, and don't give it to the dragon.

"Why not?"

"It makes him burp."

If you need anything just come and get me, I'm not a deep sleeper. One morning when I woke up I found my dragon by the side of my grass bed, looking over at me.

I said to him go back to bed, and he left the room. Sometimes I'm not sure if he knows what I'm saying, he's definitely not that's smart. I think he's a smart dragon, and I wouldn't mind him being around me.

"Can we take the chains off of him?"

“No,” I won't let anyone else do that.

It's dark outside, you must stay in now. I'll tell you both a good story, one evening I lit a torch and went out exploring. After what happened I'll never do that again.

“What happened?”

“I was attacked by the creatures of the night.”

They look like reptilians and are terrifying when you come in contact with them. Lucky for me there was a red wolf nearby, he came in and protected me and helped to escort me home. After that night my parents always locked the doors at night.

Meanwhile, a man was getting ready to start a fire. Since it was dark he had torches around him allowing him to be able to see.

He had got enough wood now and sat down on the ground by where he was going to light the fire. He picked up some small sticks and began rubbing them together.

After rubbing them together for a while, the fire started. Suddenly the flame got much larger and was beginning to take the shape of a wolf. He couldn't believe his eyes, then it began speaking to him. He stood up and ran off, before the fire wolf could see where he went. The fire wolf immediately went in the direction it thought he went.

It tore through the dark forest, causing trees and shrubs to catch fire. Most of the leaves on the forest floor were now on fire.

The fire wolf came to the Pixie sanctuary, the pixies were all settled in, and everything was quiet. The Fire wolf let out a ferocious roar, waking everything up.

It ran across a long stretch of grass, making it all catch fire. The pixies began throwing rocks and shooting spell balls at him, but this didn't slow him down at all. It saw a family of chipmunks and chased after them, they were unable to outrun the wolf and were burned up. It slammed into a sculpture, knocking it down.

It shattered into pieces, he went over to the dozens of beautiful lotus plants and blew fire out of its mouth all over them.

They went to nothing, there was a groove of fruit trees nearby.

He ran over to them and was causing havoc there. He ate some of the fruit, then set the trees on fire. There was nothing sacred left in the sanctuary.

All the pixies locked themselves in their tree homes, for safety. Where there used to be nice grass, was now just scorched ground. Then the fire wolf, saw several homes. There was no one outside to attack, so he smashed into the sides of the home, waking up the farmer who was inside. The outside of the home was now on fire.

The minute the farmer opened the door, the wolf tore the door down and swiftly devoured him. A giant nearby saw the flames and came running.

The fire wolf turned and saw the giant, he just stood there waiting for the giant to come over to him. He ran at the giant, burning his leg.

The giant angrily slammed his fists down, he kept trying to hit the wolf but was too slow.

The wolf fired fire out of it's mouth at him, causing him to lose balance and collapse. The giant got up and grabbed a fallen tree, swinging it at the wolf. It struck the wolf, throwing him into the air.

Since the tree that touched the wolf it was now on fire, the giant put it down before he burned his hands.

The wolf came back for more, it jumped onto the giants back. The giant tried to get it off his back, but the wolf kept firing fire onto the giants body.

The giant soon succumbed to the fire and collapsed. A large red bird came flying down from the nights sky, it left out a screeching sound.

It started firing blue fire out of its mouth at the wolf, he easily dodged it. It attacked with its long sharp talons but was careful not to get too close to the wolf. Once again it fired the blue fire at him while at the same time the wolf fired his fire. Then there was a huge explosion, with enough force to blow the wolf backwards into a stone pillar.

Then a giant owl flew in and landed. The wolfs fire burned out and disappeared. Both the guys had settled in for the night.

The next morning, the wizard was cooking goose eggs for breakfast. You can have eggs or just bread if you’re a picky eater. His dragon was sitting beside him, this is his favorite time.

You can pet him if you want, no we'll just leave him be. He gave the extra egg to the dragon, who quickly ate it down.

“Does he eat everything like that?”

“Yes,” he does.

I taught him how to do the dishes in the creek, and you called him dumb. He's not good on all the tasks, give him a break.

I don't mean to run out on both of you, but I need to get started on finding the fire wolf and eradicate him.

While you were both sleeping I got my stuff together, it's okay if you're not done eating just take your time and finish up.

"Do you know where we live?"

"Yes."

When I'm done slaying the wolf I'll give you a visit.

"Should we lock this place up when we leave?"

"No."

The dragon was flying around him, this is what happens when he gets excited. He waved goodbye to them and went on his way.

"Are you done eating your breakfast?"

"Yes," we need to get back before mom gets up.

It would be a miracle if we got back there that early. Before they left they made sure that the place was back in order. We have to get going now, they closed the door behind them and we're on their way. Let's run, they ran for a ways then got tired. We're almost halfway there, I'm sure you could run some more.

"Are you purposely trying to run me into the ground?"

"No."

After taking a break they ran again and soon came to their home. Their sister was watering the flowers around their house.

It's good to see you both came back early; our mother isn't feeling so well so she's still resting.

You're sorry to hear about that, I sat next to her bed watching her for a while. I would like some milk this morning so I'm going to go milk the goat. You both can come with me if you like, we'll stay here with mom. I'm sure my boyfriend will be coming over soon, I'll be back soon.

While they were resting, the wizard came upon the tracks of the fire wolf. By the looks them they were fresh, he brought out his wand. He continued following the tracks, until he came to the dark forest.

He knew that any moment the fire wolf would come out. His dragon stopped flying around and stood still beside him. That's when he knew that his dragon sensed that something was near. Suddenly the fire wolf came out of the thicket.

He pointed the wand at him and spoke the words to break the curse, but the wolf laughed at him.

You think that's going to stop me, you don't know what you're getting yourself into. That puny young dragon won't defeat me, just leave him out of this.

I'll easily knocked him out, and you and him will perish. Your parents always ran away from me, never to face me. They're not worth nothing, just weak humans.

You think you can outwit me, you're too old to make a good fighter anymore. Now I'm going to put you in your grave, we'll see about that.

I'm going to bite your wand in half and burn your old bones. I'll burn you to pieces if you say those words again, go home and take a nap.

Oh, burning soul I command you to burn out at once, gunta guna guntis muntis fire.

The fire wolf fired fire at him, they dodged the fire. He quickly began speaking the second verse, while reading the verse a tear began running down his eye.

He quickly brought up the wand besides his eye and his went onto his wand. This time when he sternly pointed it at the fire wolf, a tornado formed around the wolf and many lightning bolts came down onto him.

The fire was beginning to deplete, he tried to shoot fire at him but instead collapsed. Your time is coming to an end you evil thing, he commanded the evil spirit to leave at once, twice.

His dragon opened his mouth and shot out fire, this caused a huge explosion throwing the wizard up into the air.

His dragon caught him and gently put him down, the fire wolf was no longer there, and everyone was safe.

After resting for a while, he had enough energy to make the trip back to the boys home. When he got there everyone was standing outside, it's good to see all of you again.

"How are you doing Ma'am?"

"I'm alright."

He stayed there for a while talking to everyone, they had a great time talking. He told them how he got rid of the curse, he said his goodbyes and left, headed for home. Sometime later the king, was replaced with his successor. The pixie sanctuary had to be rebuilt, the local giants helped with that. The sorceress mystery disappeared, never to be heard from again.

www.ingramcontent.com/pod-product-compliance
Lightning Source LLC
LaVergne TN
LVHW050314160826
845677LV00014B/3383

* 9 7 9 8 8 3 7 1 9 3 8 1 1 *